**Elderpark Library**
228a Langlands Road
Glasgow G51 3TZ
Phone: 0141 276 1540 Fax 276 1541

This book is due for return on or before the last date shown below. It may
be renewed by telephone, personal application, fax or post, quoting this
date, author, title and the book number

0 6 JAN 2018 A.W'18 1 7 MAR 2018 1 0 AUG 2018 2 2 MAR 2019	WITHDRAWN	KT-381-962

Glasgow Life and its service brands, including Glasgow
Libraries, (found at www.glasgowlife.org.uk) are operating
names for Culture and Sport Glasgow

To everyone who said 'What do you really love doing?'
or 'Keep going!' – M.N.

To Carter – M.P.

Kelpies is an imprint of Floris Books
First published in 2017 by Floris Books
Text © 2017 Mike Nicholson. Illustrations © 2017 Floris Books
Mike Nicholson and Mike Phillips have asserted their rights
under the Copyright, Designs and Patent Act 1988
to be identified as the Author and Illustrator of this work

The publisher acknowledges subsidy from
Creative Scotland towards the publication
of this volume

MIX
Paper from
responsible sources
FSC
www.fsc.org   FSC® C117931

British Library CIP data available
ISBN 978-178250-362-0
Printed & bound by MBM Print SCS Ltd, Glasgow

and the Case of the
Hidden Hieroglyphics

Written by Mike Nicholson

Illustrated by Mike Phillips

Young
Kelpies

THE SQUAD

Kennedy

Nabster

Laurie

Colin the hamster

Magda Gaskar

Gus

AND FEATURING...

Prof. Peter Gyptex

Vera Damclot

Some people think that museums are boring places.

Glass cases. Old stuff. Dust.

Wrong.

Think more of

wild animals

ANCIENT MUMMIES

enormous insects

COLOURFUL COSTUMES

glittering treasure

and amazing objects found nowhere else in the world.

Then imagine that each thing in the museum has its own strange story. With secrets from the past to be uncovered. Codes to be cracked. Odd characters and their fiendish plans. Each one creating a job for a team of expert investigators:

MUSEUM MYSTERY SQUAD

In this book you will find the Squad in the depths of the museum, somewhere in a maze of corridors and stairs.

Today, like every day, they have

a puzzle to solve...

Chapter 1
In which a crossword proves to be tricky

"5 across. Building which displays interesting objects. 6 letters. Begins with 'm' and ends in 'm'."

Nabster was doing a crossword on the laptop. The puzzle appeared on the big interactive smartboard at the same time.

It was a lazy day in the Museum Mystery Squad's headquarters. Kennedy was writing in her diary (as usual) and Laurie was dozing in his sleeping bag on the sofa (as usual).

"Mmmmm," said Nabster thoughtfully, as he span around slowly on his chair. "6 letters, begins with 'm' and ends in 'm'."

Laurie gave a big yawn and rolled over. He blinked up at the screen through his large glasses, which were partly covered by his floppy fringe.

"How about a different word. Six letters. Clue: not very clever. Begins with 'n-u-m' and ends in 'p-t-y'."

"How does that help me?" asked Nabster.

Laurie sighed. "What was *your* clue again?"

"Building which contains interesting objects. Begins with 'm' and ends in 'm'," repeated Nabster.

Laurie groaned in despair. "It's MUSEUM, you fool! You know, like the one you're sitting in!"

"Ohhhh yeeeeah!" said Nabster, a slow grin splitting

across his face as he typed in the answer.

"You've got five still to do," said Laurie glancing at the screen. "The answers are FIREPLACE, SALT, EXTRA, TOOTH and BINGO." He rolled back to his previous position as if he was about to doze again.

Nabster was open-mouthed. "How does he do that?" he asked Kennedy.

"Looks at the answers, I bet," she replied. "Oi!" said the lumpy sleeping bag on the sofa. "I can't help being a genius even when I'm asleep."

Nabster started typing Laurie's suggestions into the crossword. "I like puzzles," he said happily.

"Me too," said Kennedy. "I wish we had another case to work on."

"Yeah, no mystery could remain unsolved with Nabster here to unravel the clues," muttered Laurie sarcastically.

Kennedy, Nabster and Laurie were, in actual fact, a team of expert investigators: the Museum Mystery Squad. Whenever there was a secret to uncover or a strange story to investigate, the Museum Director Magda Gaskar asked for their help.

Each Squad member had different skills. Mohammed McNab or 'Nabster' was the technical and computing expert. He could also take apart and re-make any gadget (even though he couldn't work out that 'museum' was a six letter word beginning and ending in 'm' when he was sitting inside one).

Laurie Lennox's speciality was asking very direct

questions (even though he seemed to spend half his life asleep).

Kennedy Kerr worked at high speed and often connected ideas that seemed totally random to everyone else (even though she often didn't stand still long enough to explain her thinking).

Oh, and not forgetting Colin: the hamster in the cage in the corner of the room.

You might think that a hamster is not the fiercest of guard dogs or the most glamorous of animals to work alongside a team of investigators. And you'd be right. But Colin had carved out his place in the team by coming up with vital new ways of thinking about a case, only possible from a hamster's-eye view (even though most of his thoughts were about carrots, straw and sleep).

Honestly, it's true. Wait and see.

Just as Nabster was completing the final crossword answer, there was a PING! from his laptop. A ping doesn't sound like much. (In fact it just sounds like a ping.) But this tiny noise often marked the start of an adventure for the Museum Mystery Squad.

It was the sound of an email arriving.

Nabster read the message.

"Oh good!" he said with a grin. "Wakey-wakey Laurie."

"I *am* awake," said the horizontal lump, before gently snoring again.

"It looks like our next case has arrived," Nabster continued.

Kennedy stopped writing her diary and looked up at the screen.

To: **MMS@museums.co.uk**
Subject: Code to solve

Dear Kennedy, Laurence and Mohammed,

A researcher examining one of our exhibits, an Egyptian casket, has just uncovered some hieroglyphics that haven't been seen since ancient times.

This is an important discovery right under our roof. I'm heading to the Egyptian Zone now. Can you meet me there shortly at 11.00 a.m.?

It would be good to get as many minds as possible decoding the hieroglyphics.

Thank you as ever,

Magda Gaskar
Museum Director

"The Egyptian Zone," said Nabster. "That's where children can drop off a parent, isn't it?"

It was Laurie's turn to look confused, but Kennedy worked it out.

"Ha! Yeah, that's right. It's a special room for mummies!"

Chapter 2
In which a very long
word is introduced

"There are some new what?" asked Laurie, after Nabster had read out the email again.

"Hieroglyphics," replied Kennedy.

"Higher-o what?"

"Hi-er-o-glyph-ics," Kennedy said slowly. "A set of symbols used like writing. You know, in ancient Egypt. Carvings in pyramids?"

"So instead of a sentence you write a set of little pictures?"

"Exactly. A bit like telling a story using only emojis, no words."

There was a minute's delay while Nabster tried to type:

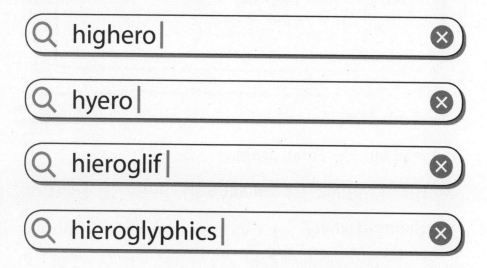

Q highero| ⊗

Q hyero| ⊗

Q hieroglif| ⊗

Q hieroglyphics| ⊗

He found an example and showed it on the smartboard.

Laurie sat up. "Why are there strange-looking people with bird heads, and big weird eyes?" he asked.

"Watch what you say. Have you looked in the mirror recently?" asked Nabster.

"Ha ha, very funny," said Laurie. "Seriously though... what does it all mean?"

"I think each symbol represents a word," said Kennedy. "See what else you can find out, Nabster."

Fifteen minutes later the team were all a lot clearer about hieroglyphics.

FACT FILE

HIEROGLYPHICS

* Each picture stands for an object, action, sound or idea

* There are 26 letters in our alphabet but over 700 Egyptian hieroglyphic symbols

* There is no punctuation in hieroglyphics

* The word comes from two Greek words: *hieros* meaning holy and *glyphe* meaning writing: holy-writing

* No one could read hieroglyphics for hundreds of years until a carved stone called the Rosetta Stone was translated in 1822

* Hieroglyphics can be read vertically, horizontally, left to right, or right to left depending on the instruction given

"This is cool," said Nabster. "I might start writing in symbols instead of words."

"You might make more sense that way," said Laurie.

Nabster drew two laughing faces.

"What's that?" asked Laurie.

"It says, 'Ha ha'!" replied Nabster.

"Imagine life without punctuation," said Kennedy.

itwouldbereallyharddontyouthinktomakeoutwhat
peoplewritesaidlaurie

"That's how Colin communicates when he runs over my keyboard," said Nabster. "Not a full stop, comma or even a space in sight!"

Kennedy looked at her watch. "We should get going. Here's another puzzle: how many seconds are in five minutes?"

"Three hundred," replied Laurie. "Why?"

"That's how long we have until Magda is expecting us in the Egyptian Zone."

As usual, Kennedy was almost out of the door even while she was suggesting leaving. She thought and moved fast. Nabster had often wondered about creating a human-sized version of Colin's hamster wheel to tire Kennedy out. That way she might walk at a more normal speed when they had to go somewhere together.

"Wait for us!" he called. He was sorting out equipment in his bag, removing the less useful items and replacing them with what he might need for gathering information.

sweet wrappers (empty) ✗

paper clip (bent) ✗

sock (why?) ✗

string ✓

measuring tape ✓

notebook and pen ✓

dictionary of Egyptian phrases ✓

camera ✓

the ScanRay (best gadget ever) ✓

Colin

Meanwhile Laurie was deciding what to wear from his wardrobe rail. When he wasn't in his sleeping bag, Laurie had a huge selection of clothes to choose from. You never quite knew what was coming next, but somehow he always looked cool – in a Laurie Lennox sort of way. On this occasion he chose a khaki-coloured shirt, baggy trousers, battered boots and an old wide-brimmed hat. "You look like Indiana Jones," said Nabster.

"Exactly," said Laurie. "I'm all set for the Egyptian Zone. No hieroglyphics will defeat me!"

Nabster grabbed his pen and notebook and scribbled:

"Writing in pictures! It means: Let's go!"

With that, the team were off to crack an ancient code.

Chapter 3
In which some ancient writing is uncovered

Kennedy, Laurie and Nabster ran through the maze of corridors in the basement of the museum.

The Museum Mystery Squad headquarters was far from public view. The way to the main display halls was long and twisting: down fifteen stairs then up twelve stairs, round five different corners and along six corridors – all of which looked exactly the same.

The three Squad members knew the complicated route like the backs of their hands. But anyone who didn't know the way usually got very lost, unless they had a long ball of string trailing after them (unlikely) or had left a trail of breadcrumbs (very unlikely).

The doorway to the Egyptian Zone had two towering pillars of sandstone, as if marking the entrance to a chamber within a pyramid.

In the first room, the team found display cases that burst with colour. These held jewellery covered in sparkling blue, red and green gems. (Laurie's attention was immediately taken by these. You could see he was eyeing them up for a future outfit.)

At the centre of the display was a golden headdress studded with the most striking precious stones. The information board in the display case declared that this was Pharaoh Shaneb's headdress, one of the museum's greatest treasures. It had been entombed with the pharaoh after he died.

"It says here that hieroglyphic records suggest there were two bracelets that matched this headdress, which would have been amazing to see, but they aren't in this museum. In fact, only one of them has ever been found," read Kennedy.

The next room in the Egyptian Zone seemed filled with gold. In the centre was the zone's most dramatic piece: the golden mummy casket of Pharaoh Shaneb.

The huge container was decorated with a larger-than-life body that had its arms crossed over its chest. Enormous eyes stared out from the gleaming face. The sides of the container were covered in hieroglyphics –

similar pictures and symbols to the ones the team had been looking at on their smartboard just a short while before.

Three people were already there looking closely at the casket.

There was the tall thin figure of Gus the security guard, who often helped the Squad when they were solving mysteries. Magda Gaskar the museum director was there. And a third person who they didn't know,

was crouched beside the mummy casket: a grey-haired man with glasses, concentrating so hard on what he was doing that he didn't seem to notice the Squad as they approached.

The Egyptian Zone was closed to museum visitors for a few days while the room was being repainted, so it was all quiet, apart from a man painting on scaffolding at the far side of the room.

"Hello you three," called Magda cheerfully. "I thought you would all be keen to see this. Even though this casket has been in our collection for years, we've just discovered something very interesting. I'd welcome your thoughts on it."

The man peering at the casket glanced round, looked over the top of his spectacles and gave the team a nod and a smile. "You must be the bright sparks that I've been hearing about."

"I'd like you to meet Professor Peter Gyptex," said Magda. "He researches ancient Egypt. He was looking at the pharaoh's casket and has made the most amazing discovery."

"It's a secret message," Gus chipped in. "From thousands of years ago."

The team peered around Professor Gyptex to get a better view. A patch was missing from the surface of the casket, about the size and thickness of a slice of toast. It looked like a small piece of the outer layer had been lifted off. The same shape lay beside the container.

"It's quite possibly the first time this message has been seen for thousands of years," said the professor. "We'll need to be very careful."

"How did that little panel come off?" asked Laurie, going for the direct question as usual.

The professor carried on looking closely at the casket as he answered. "Quite by accident," he explained. "I was examining the surface when I must have pressed something to release it."

"I was walking past when it happened," added Gus.

"The thing sprang off and landed with a clatter. I thought the painter was throwing things at me at first!"

"Maybe he'd heard some of your jokes," said Nabster quietly. Gus told the worst jokes ever.

But it wasn't a missile from the painter. Even from where they stood, the team could see the symbols that had been revealed where the panel had fallen off. A secret message in ancient hieroglyphics had been hidden underneath the surface of the casket, until now.

Chapter 4
In which a cat stays very still indeed

Professor Gyptex stood up fully, as though unfolding his lanky body after crouching by the casket. He faced the team. "Hieroglyphics often say quite simple things. Sometimes it's just a little personal message. Like a note scrawled in the back of a school jotter or a line of graffiti on a wall. Interesting but not important."

"Are these secret symbols new ones or ones you've seen before?" As ever, Laurie's questions were short and to the point.

"A cat, an eye, a hand. Usual sort of stuff," said the professor in a casual way. "You see they are very similar to these ones here." He pointed to a long line of symbols on the side of the casket. "I'll do a few comparisons with other messages and should have a translation in a few days."

"Oh well," said Magda. "It sounds like there's less of a mystery than I had thought, but it's interesting to have something new revealed here in the museum."

"We'll have a look anyway. We were just saying that we like having a puzzle to solve." Kennedy nodded to Nabster, signalling to him to take a photo. Nabster rummaged in his bag for a camera.

Professor Gyptex was standing close to the casket and cast a big shadow over the newly discovered symbols.

"Perhaps I should just put the little panel back on

36

for safety at the moment," he said. "We don't want any harm done. After all, this surface hasn't been exposed to the light for thousands of years."

"I'll just get a quick photo and then you can cover it up again." Nabster eased his way round the professor and took a few quick snaps.

"How did you become an Egypt expert?" Laurie continued with his string of questions.

Professor Gyptex looked surprised to be asked. "Em…
Well, I probably got interested in Egypt when I was
about your age. When I was older I travelled there –
took a trip along the River Nile – visited the pyramids
and the Sphinx."

"Wow! I'd love to go to Egypt and see the Sphinx,"
said Kennedy.

"Oh yes – it's quite a sight – an enormous lion's
head on a human body! Quite breathtaking."

"Look at that!" Nabster gasped. He had stepped back
from taking photos and was now completely focused
on the exhibit next to the golden mummy casket.
This figure wasn't human. It was a bundle of wrapped
bandages, topped by the shape of a cat's head, which
had staring eyes.

"Never mind 'Look at that!'. You should be saying '**What** is that?'" said Laurie, pointing at the odd creature.

"It's like a mummy but it's a cat!" said Kennedy.

"That's exactly right," Magda confirmed. "The ancient Egyptians were very fond of their pets. They gave them the same treatment as kings and queens when they died.

They wrapped them up and preserved them."

"That is officially one of the weirdest things I have ever seen," said Laurie. He leaned in and gazed hard at it through his big glasses. "Its eyes are really spooky."

"You can talk." Nabster grinned at his floppy-fringed friend.

"Good heavens is that the time?" They were interrupted by Professor Gyptex. He was checking an enormous watch on his wrist and began rushing to pack up his equipment. "I need to head off now." He swiftly popped the little toast-size panel back into place on the casket, hiding the message once more.

Nabster wasn't bothered, as he had his photos already. He was more excited by the mummified cat. He took his very favourite gadget, the ScanRay, from his bag and checked its controls. Shaped like a supermarket hand scanner, the ScanRay took readings of any object and then listed what it was made of. In the past it had given the Squad vital mystery-solving information.*

When Professor Gyptex saw what Nabster was doing, his departure plans changed. He seemed to find the ScanRay much more interesting than his giant wristwatch.

"Goodness me," he said. "I haven't seen a piece of kit like that before. Is it some kind of material scanning device?" He stared intently at the gadget in Nabster's hands.

"It's a ScanRay," said Nabster. "It tells you what something is made of. Sort of like an x-ray but without the picture. It's helped us on lots of our cases."

* See *Museum Mystery Squad and the Case of the Moving Mammoth*

"Nabster wouldn't go anywhere without it," said Kennedy. "You're lucky he hasn't scanned you already!"

"Ha ha ha, how amusing... I'm not sure you'd find much of interest about me, but I can see how it could be very useful," said Professor Gyptex slowly, still completely distracted from his rush to get away.

To show how brilliantly it worked, Nabster held the ScanRay close to the surface of the pharaoh's casket and switched it on. Seconds later the readout showed:

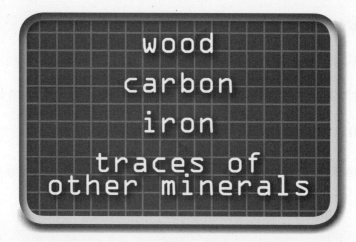

wood
carbon
iron
traces of
other minerals

"The museum emptied the casket long ago to study the mummy itself and all Pharaoh Shaneb's jewels and precious possessions," said Magda Gaskar.

"That's why there's no **dead body** on the readout," said Nabster. "The ScanRay is picking up what the casket and its ancient paint are made of."

Taking a few steps to the side, he held his gadget towards the mummified cat. There was a bleep as the readout appeared.

"Could I see that?" Professor Gyptex reached over to take the ScanRay. "Fascinating... fascinating piece of equipment." He held it up, turned it around and upside down. He switched it off as he handed it back to Nabster. "Very interesting indeed. Thank you for the demonstration. Probably best not to use this on objects as ancient and valuable as these." He indicated the casket and the cat and addressed Magda Gaskar as he did so. "It would be a shame to spoil such precious items with any harmful rays."

Nabster looked shocked. No one had ever questioned the ScanRay before or suggested that it might be doing any damage.

Magda considered the Egyptian expert's opinion, and nodded in agreement: Nabster's scanner was not to be used in the Egyptian Zone.

WHAT WOULD YOU TAKE WITH YOU?

The Squad have discovered that the cat and the golden headdress were just two of the objects found in Pharaoh Shaneb's tomb. Egyptian pharaohs filled their tombs with all the things they needed in the afterlife.

LOADS OF FOOD

It's a long journey to the afterlife. The pharaoh needed enough food, water and wine to feed him and all his servants.

A SARCOPHAGUS

Pharaohs wanted to preserve their bodies for the afterlife so not only were they mummified, they were placed inside wooden coffins, inside a sarcophagus (a stone or gold coffin).

JEWELLERY

Just like Laurie, pharaohs want to look good, wherever they are going. They were buried with lots of treasure: gold amulets, bracelets and gems.

BOAT AND CART

Pharaohs don't walk anywhere – not even in the afterlife!

A MUMMIFIED CROCODILE

All the cool pharoahs have one! Mummified crocodiles were often preserved with gold and precious jewels.

STATUES

Who will make the food or row the boat? Pharoahs thought they would need servants. They buried small statues, which they believed would become real in the afterlife.

If you were a pharaoh, what 3 things would be on your wish list?

1. _____

2. _____

3. _____

Chapter 5
In which a puzzle is puzzling

<u>Kennedy's Diary</u>

Tuesday, 12 noon

Puzzles = Fun.

<u>This</u> puzzle = Not sure.

We don't have to peer round a professor now: we've got Nabster's photos of the casket's secret message on the big smartboard screen in the HQ, but it still doesn't make much sense.

A hand, an eye, a cat, a squiggle or two

→ pretty random...

If only the ancient Egyptians had used emojis.

"Maybe we should stick to crosswords," said Nabster, looking at the photo of the uncovered hieroglyphics on the smartboard.

"It must mean something to somebody," said Laurie. "Especially since it was a message that was hidden away."

"According to the professor, it could just be somebody's scribbles," said Kennedy, peering at the image as if staring at it harder would explain what it meant.

"Maybe it just says 'Pharaoh was here'," said Nabster.

"From the look of the symbols it's more like 'Pharaoh's cat was here'," said Laurie. "What is it with these ancient Egyptians and their cats? Can you imagine treating your dead pet like that?"

They glanced over at Colin who was running on the hamster wheel in his cage. It was hard to imagine him bound up in bandages and staring out at them all with spooky eyes.

They all looked blankly at the hieroglyphic symbols for a while longer.

"Maybe it's just a message about the cat," said Kennedy. "I love my cat?"

"That would surely be this." Nabster drew a few symbols on a scrap of paper:

"But the casket's secret message has a picture of a hand in it as well," said Laurie. "It could be more like 'I love to hold and look at my cat'. That was probably true for the Pharaoh if he liked cats. But why hide a secret message saying that? What else could it mean?"

The team began to make a list of possible meanings on the smartboard.

Look! My cat's got no hands.

Please look after my cat.

If you see this cat, hold onto it.

I own a one-eyed cat.

See this cat? It's handy.

"What else do we know about that casket?" asked Laurie, deciding they needed a different angle.

Nabster did a quick internet search and soon had the results up beside their list on the board. "This is one of the best examples of an ancient Egyptian casket," he read. "It was made for the Pharaoh Shaneb nearly three thousand years ago."

"This also mentions the priceless headdress that we saw in the display case," said Kennedy. "The one that used to be in the casket with the mummy. Along with lots of jewels."

"That jewellery was amazing," said Laurie. "I wonder if Magda would let me borrow some. What's the right occasion to dress up as a pharaoh? Fancy dress party? Burns Night? Halloween?"

"Since when did you wait for a special day to wear crazy clothes?" asked Nabster.

The image on the screen changed to a photo of a wonderful bracelet. It was wide enough to go round someone's wrist and some way up their arm too. The golden gleam made it appear valuable, and so did the rows of gems round the edges.

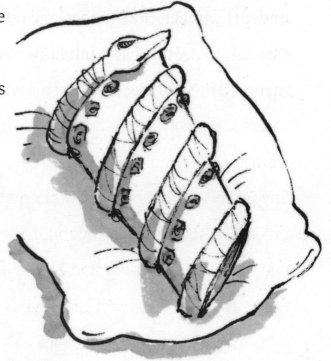

"Wow, look at those! The red ones must be rubies," said Kennedy.

"And the green ones will be emeralds," said Nabster. "That's some bracelet!"

"I didn't see that upstairs. Is it here?" asked Laurie. "I want to go back up and take a look."

"No, it's not here," said Kennedy, reading the text under the image. "Remember, the notice on the display case said that the Pharaoh had two bracelets that matched the headdress. After this one came out of the casket it was lent to a museum in Paris, but it was stolen from there six months ago. And I don't think there's any point searching for the other one. There are two bracelets shown in drawings of Shaneb, but the second one wasn't in the casket and has never been found. It hasn't been seen since the days when they were building pyramids and mummifying cats."

"Who stole the first bracelet from the Paris museum?" asked Laurie. "Did the French police catch the thief?" As he asked the question he put on a large colourful necklace, which had been hanging on the end of his wardrobe rail. All this talk of jewellery was giving him ideas.

Nabster found a newspaper article about the Paris theft and displayed it on the wall screen.

PARIS MUSEUM THEFT

PRICELESS EGYPTIAN ARTEFACT MISSING WITHOUT TRACE

The whereabouts of a world-famous bracelet are unknown after two thieves stole it from a Paris museum. CCTV images show one culprit is a man who pretended to be a painter redecorating the room where items of Pharaoh Shaneb's jewellery were on display. It appears that after taking the bracelet from the display case, the man hid it in the museum's toilets, before it was collected and removed from the building by his accomplice – an unidentified woman. One line of enquiry is that the pair of thieves could be brother and sister as CCTV images suggest the two thieves look alike.

"We must find this pair of criminals so we can recover Shaneb's valuable and fascinating ancient bracelet for all to enjoy," said the Paris museum's director, Mozam Bique.

"Is anyone thinking what I'm thinking?" asked Laurie. "A thief disguised as a *painter*..."

57

DECODE HIEROGLYPHICS

Egyptian hieroglyphics don't have an alphabet like ours. Hieroglyphics can be symbols, or pictures of animals, people or objects. Some are easy to figure out, some confusing and some impossible!

Nabster has been making up his own picture and symbol messages. Can you figure out what they mean?

1.

2.

3.

4.

5.

6.

Answers at the back of the book

Chapter 6
In which someone purrs

Kennedy and Nabster understood immediately
what Laurie was thinking. If the Paris museum's
thief had been disguised as a painter, then could
that happen here? Just who was the man they had
seen quietly painting upstairs in the Egyptian Zone?
Was he genuine? Had he ever been in Paris? Was
one of their own museum's exhibits about to be
stolen?!

The Museum Mystery Squad's ideas and questions
came thick and fast.

"What if the painter upstairs is the same pretend painter from Paris?"

"He could be after that golden headdress!"

"Or maybe he's poking around, hoping to find the matching bracelet..."

"...the one that's been missing since ancient times."

"Back to the Egyptian Zone, everyone!"

But as soon as they arrived in the Egyptian Zone, the Squad could see that the painter was no longer there. The scaffolding was empty. All the paint pots and rollers and sheets for catching drips had been tidied away.

They were looking at each other, wondering what to do next, when there was a whistle and a wave from over by Pharaoh Shaneb's casket. Gus the security guard was

61

standing there with the mummified cat and a rather unusual guest.

"Hello team," said Gus. "I'd like you to meet a friend of Professor Gyptex. This is Vera Damclot, and she has a... a very particular interest in mummified cats."

Vera was a bit peculiar. She was tall and gangly and wearing a cardigan that went down to her knees. On the back was a giant knitted picture of a cat.

"Hallo my de-e-e-ars," she said. "Have you come to see this da-a-a-arling little cat?" Her voice was low and seemed to purr as she talked.

They nodded. It was too complicated to explain that they were actually here to spy on the museum's painter and decorator.

Vera was wearing special plastic handling-gloves and was cradling the mummified cat as if it was a tiny baby. As she moved around, the Squad members noticed that her leggings had pictures of kittens with enormous eyes on them, and she was wearing dangly cat-shaped earrings. They quickly got the idea. Vera loved cats. Madly.

Gus took a step behind Vera's tall figure. He raised his eyebrows up very high and twirled his finger next to his ear to indicate this person was as loopy as the bandages wrapped around a mummy.

"It's so-o-o-o good to be here. What a deli-i-i-ight to see this incr-r-r-redible cat." The odd woman looked down at the cat in her arms. It was almost disappearing up her baggy cardigan sleeve. "Did you kno-o-o-w this wonderful cre-e-e-ature is going to inspire a new generation of cat lover-r-r-r-rs?"

Kennedy, Laurie and Nabster all looked a bit blank, so Gus helped with an explanation.

"Vera thinks that turning things into mummies might be an idea from ancient history which is worth bringing back in the present day."

Before he could say any more, Vera Damclot chipped in. "Those ancient Egyptians kne-e-e-w how to look after their cats. They gave them pr-r-r-ride of place." Her cardigan flapped as she spoke, the

64

mummified cat almost smothered by her loving hugs. "We can lear-r-r-rn from how they tr-r-r-eated their dear-r-r-r departed feline fr-r-r-riends and do the same toda-a-a-y."

"What... mummify cats? Why exactly would you do that?" asked Laurie, as direct as ever.

Vera peered at the Indiana Jones lookalike as if he had landed from another planet.

"Why my de-e-e-ar-r-r-r boy... Then we could keep our-r-r-r cats for-r-r-rever!"

Gus explained further. "Vera has been researching how the Egyptians wrapped up their cats' bodies after they died. She thinks cat owners today will all want to do the same once she shows them how."

"Yes, I've been learning the tr-r-r-ricks of their tr-r-r-rade.

So simple yet so clever. I'm going to pr-r-r-ractise at home and then tell cat owners ar-r-r-round the country how to do it." Vera Damclot gently replaced the mummified cat, bending low to position it with as much care as possible. She removed her protective gloves and tucked them in her cardigan pocket. "Well, I shall take my le-e-e-eave of you," she said. "That's been most helpfu-u-u-ul. I've got so many ideas I'm fit to bur-r-r-rst!"

"So have you really learnt enough about mummifying pets just from looking at that cat?" asked Laurie.

"Well I am also doing lots of r-r-r-reading and r-r-r-research," purred the woman. "If you'll excuse me I'm keen to spend a little time in the computer-r-r-r room here. We are so-o-o-o lucky to live in this modern age and yet be able to lear-r-r-rn from the pa-a-a-a-ast."

With that, the strange cat woman walked off. She gave a backwards wave without turning as she strode out to a corridor that led past toilets towards the computers in the museum's Interactive Learning Zone.

"She's not just catty, she's totally batty," said Laurie. He looked closely at her clothes as she left. There was certainly nothing she had on that would suit a Laurie Lennox outfit.

"She's almost as odd as that bug-eyed cat," said Kennedy, picking up a piece of thread from the floor. It seemed to have come from the bandages of the mummified moggy. There was a light trail of dust on the floor too, perhaps just because the cat had been moved.

Gus shook his head. "Weird. Just weird. Professor Gyptex seemed to think she was all right. She had a letter of introduction from him, saying that she would take great care with the cat. Magda was amused that Vera wants to bring back the art of making mummies. Anyway, talking of funny things," Gus went on, "here's one for you: what music do mummies like?"

The Squad looked blank as Gus grinned, delighted with the punchline that was coming: "Rap! Get it?

Rap – wrap. Because mummies are all *wrapped* up in bandages, you see?"

There were three polite smiles from the Museum Mystery Squad. Gus had actually cracked a better joke than usual. With Vera Damclot gone, the team told Gus they were looking for the painter who had been redecorating the Egyptian Zone.

"The decorator? Why? He's finished his first coat of paint in here. He's off to the Animal Zone next."

That was all they needed to know. Without stopping to explain, the Squad took off running, but they had got no further than the giant stone pillars at the door of the Egyptian Zone when they saw their target up ahead.

"That's him!" said Kennedy urgently.

A figure in white overalls was heading through a fire escape door at the far end of the corridor. Whatever he was carrying looked suspiciously like a bundle of bandages.

"Is it a mummy? What's he got wrapped up?"

"He's getting away!"

"After him!"

Chapter 7
In which there is some confusion about Paris

The Squad burst through the fire exit door following the painter. He was one flight of stairs below them, heading for the ground floor, another door and the outside world. Escape was just moments away.

The Squad put on a surge of speed and caught up fast.

"Got you!" shouted Nabster. "Stop right there!"

The man looked up, startled. "Er... OK," he said.

"We know what you did in Paris!" declared Kennedy.

"That's very clever of you," said the man, seeming slightly confused.

"Ah, so you admit you were there?" Kennedy was triumphant.

"I was there on holiday with my wife last year," said the man. "How did you know?"

"A-ha! A man and a woman!" said Kennedy. "Just as we suspected."

"Er... yes," said the painter. "We often go on holiday together... Isn't that normal?"

"What did you do with the bracelet?" demanded Laurie.

"Now you've lost me," said the man.

"Where do you think you're taking that mummy?" asked Laurie.

Everyone's attention turned to the bundle of bandages in the painter's arms.

"Excuse me?" The man was looking more and more confused as the conversation went on.

"Put it down," said Nabster. His voice had an accusing tone.

The man glanced at the bundle in his arms, then laid it carefully on the floor.

"My dustsheets," he said innocently. "I'm just taking them outside for a shake."

The Squad stared at the pile of paint-spattered material.

They weren't bandages.

It wasn't a mummy.

There wasn't anything in the pile but old sheets.

The man broke into a smile. "So what am I supposed to have done? I promise I was on my best behaviour in Paris. And as far as I know my wife didn't steal anything either. Now, whose mum is missing?"

At that moment Gus came through the door and joined them in the stairway. The Squad tried to explain what they'd read in the newspaper article and why they'd been suspicious of the painter.

It turned out that Gus had known Andy the painter-decorator for years. "He's one of the most honest people I've ever met," he said. "Mind you, didn't you paint the police station once, Andy? That means you had a brush with the law... *Brush*, get it? You know, paintbrush?"

"I did spill a lot of maroon paint there," said Andy. "I got caught red-handed!"

He and Gus laughed at each other's jokes while the Squad looked on. It was bad enough having Gus cracking dodgy one-liners, but now there were two of them at it.

Kennedy, Nabster and Laurie headed downstairs. The attempt to catch their main suspect was well and truly over.

"That was so awkward," mumbled Nabster, once they were slumped together on the sofa back at the HQ.

"Talk about jumping to conclusions," said Kennedy. "I can't believe I said 'We know what you did in Paris.'"

"I can't believe we thought his dustsheets were a mummy," said Laurie gloomily.

After a few minutes of silence they each quietly returned to their usual activities – diary (Kennedy), laptop (Nabster), dreamland (Laurie).

Kennedy's Diary

Tuesday, 2:00 p.m.

Cringe - I don't think I could look at Andy the painter again without dying of embarrassment, even though he was very nice about it all.

For once Laurie's got the best idea - I think I'd quite like to be deep asleep just now!

Kennedy glanced over at Colin to see what the fourth member of the Squad was up to. "You're lucky, Colin," she said. "It's an easy life for you."

Colin sat on the straw amidst some new climbing blocks. With the Egyptian Zone in mind, Kennedy thought that he looked like a furry sphinx between some tiny pyramids.

"Hold on a minute," she said, still looking at Colin. "Something's not right... I'm not so sure Peter Gyptex really is such an Egypt expert after all."

"What makes you say that? He seemed to know his stuff," said Nabster. "And he is a professor."

"Well, he says he is, but I'm just realising he made one very big blunder. He said that the sphinx was a lion's head on a human body. I've just twigged. It's actually the other way round. It's a human head on a lion's body. No Egypt expert would get that wrong."

↑
Sphinx

↑
Not a Sphinx

"Couldn't he just have made a simple mistake?" asked Nabster.

"Maybe," said Kennedy doubtfully. "But just supposing he wasn't the expert he claims to be. Why would he be interested in the casket?"

"He certainly wasn't very keen on anyone else getting a close look at it." Laurie had woken up and quickly got up to speed.

"It was the same with the ScanRay," said Nabster, still annoyed that his prized piece of kit had been dismissed. "He switched it off before anyone saw the results."

Kennedy frowned, thinking hard. "I wonder what he didn't want us to see?"

"Well, now I think about it, I should be able to

find the data from the mummified cat," said Nabster, reaching into his bag. "The ScanRay stores the last few scans in its memory."

The team all looked at each other. This was worth checking out.

Nabster switched on the ScanRay and pressed a few buttons to get into the gadget's memory.

Laurie waited patiently, lying back on the sofa. Kennedy, however, had started to fidget, hopping from one foot to the other. This was a sure sign that she felt they were on to something.

Nabster concentrated on the ScanRay screen. "Where is it, where is it... Ah, here we go," he said. His face changed as he read. "Oh... oh... that is VERY interesting."

He turned the gadget towards Laurie and Kennedy.

"What!?" said Kennedy.

The ScanRay read-out from the mummified cat showed what they could have predicted:

cotton

organic matter

salt and spices

Those were all explained by the bandages, the dead cat and the ingredients that would have been used to mummify the moggy. But the screen also showed something no one was expecting:

Laurie asked the question. "Why is there gold in a dead cat?"

He looked up at the smartboard, where Nabster's photo of the casket's secret message was back on display.

His eyes narrowed. He moved a lazy hand up to lift his fringe and stared harder. Then in the blink of an eye he stood bolt upright.

"Wow, that's a new personal best," said Nabster. "I've never seen you move so fast."

"That's it!" cried Laurie. "That message is so simple. We should have worked that out!"

"What?" asked Nabster. "I still don't see what it means."

"Those hieroglyphics are directions. They're a secret message about where *the second gold bracelet* is hidden. The one that's never been found. A picture of a hand wearing a bracelet, a cat, and an eye to tell you to look closely. It says:

'THE BRACELET IS IN THE CAT – LOOK!'"

"Brilliant!" said Nabster, punching the air in glee.

Kennedy grinned too, but her mind was already working other things out. "If we know that, then maybe the so-called professor does too!"

FACT OR FICTION?

Kennedy is putting together a fact file to help the Squad solve this mystery. Can you help her decide whether each of these statements is TRUE or FALSE?

1. Hieroglyphics means "holy writings" in ancient Greek.
   TRUE or FALSE?

2. A sphinx is a creature from ancient Egyptian mythology with the head of a lion and the body of a human.
   TRUE or FALSE?

3. The Great Pyramid at Giza took 10,000 people 10 years to build.
   TRUE or FALSE?

4. Cats were very important in ancient Egypt. The Egyptian cat goddess was called Bastet.
TRUE or FALSE?

5. Most ancient Egyptian tombs had false entrances to stop robbers finding their precious contents.
TRUE or FALSE?

6.
is the hieroglyphic symbol for sand.
TRUE or FALSE?

Answers at the back of the book

Chapter 8
In which mixing up some letters gives interesting results

The Museum Mystery Squad charged through the corridors. They wanted to get back to the Egyptian Zone as quickly as possible. They called Gus on the walkie-talkie as they ran and asked him to meet them at the casket. He would need to know what they'd discovered.

"It's so obvious," Kennedy shouted over her shoulder to Nabster and Laurie as she sprinted. "The pharaoh left his favourite jewellery with his favourite pet."

The ScanRay and the hieroglyphics were telling

them the same thing: the Pharaoh's second bracelet had been inside the mummified cat – encased in a museum exhibit – since ancient times.

Rounding the last corner before the Egyptian Zone, the three friends just managed to stop before they ran into Gus.

"Woah! Slow down! Slow down!"

"The missing second bracelet is in the cat!"

"We cracked the code and the ScanRay tells us we're right!"

"But we think Gyptex might have solved the hieroglyphics too!"

The team quickly explained what they thought was happening, including their suspicion that Peter Gyptex might not be a real professor.

"Well, I haven't seen him back again," said Gus. "The only person interested in the cat has been Vera Damclot."

"But she's a friend of the 'professor', isn't she?" asked Laurie.

Kennedy slapped her head in frustration.

"PARIS!" she shouted.

"Paris? What's Paris got to do with anything?" said Gus.

TOILETS

"Is this some kind of new game?" he added cheerfully. "I'm quite good on my capital cities."

"Oh no, not Paris again," said Nabster. "Last time it got a mention, it was VERY embarrassing."

"Who stole the bracelet in Paris?" asked Kennedy.

"You *know* who it was," said Nabster. "A decorator. But you also know that Andy, who is doing the painting here, is exactly that! Not a thief."

"Yes, the painter idea led us the wrong way," said Kennedy. "What I mean about the Paris theft is that the newspaper said it was a man and a woman working together."

"Peter... and Vera?" said Laurie.

"Exactly," said Kennedy. "We already think that the Egypt expert isn't quite what he seems.

So what about that mad cat lover. Is she for real?"

The normally laid-back Laurie began to look slightly strange. In fact it was as though he'd been given an electric shock. His eyes widened behind his big glasses and his hands started to shake.

"PEN AND PAPER!"

"Is this the day for shouting out random things?" Gus was struggling to keep up with the Squad's thinking.

Nabster wasted no time. He grabbed a notebook and pen from his bag and thrust them at Laurie.

"What did you say a moment ago?" Laurie was poised and ready to write.

"I said that the Egypt expert and the mad cat lover were a bit unbelievable." Kennedy moved closer to see what Laurie was doing.

Laurie quickly scribbled down:

EGYPT EXPERT

on one side of the page. Further over he wrote:

MAD CAT LOVER

"Hieroglyphics... puzzles... anagrams..." he muttered. Laurie began to cross out each letter and then write them on the line below in a different order, forming new words. When he had finished he held up the sheet for the others to see.

He had spelled out Peter and Vera's names.

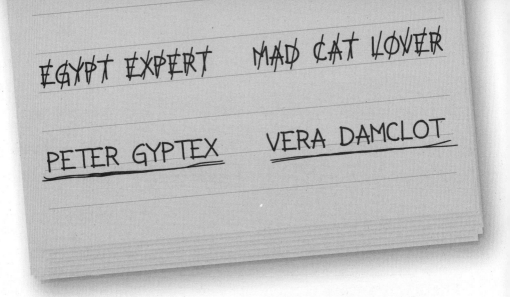

EGYPT EXPERT   MAD CAT LOVER

PETER GYPTEX   VERA DAMCLOT

"What have you done?" Nabster was puzzled by
the puzzle.

"PETER GYPTEX is an *anagram* of EGYPT EXPERT,
and VERA DAMCLOT is an anagram of MAD CAT LOVER.
They're the same letters just mixed up a different way."

"Why have Peter Gyptex and Vera Damclot both got
names like that?" asked Nabster.

"Because they're made-up names," said Laurie. "They
are not who they say they are."

Chapter 9
In which a jacket is lumpy

There was a stunned silence. Facts were now freefalling fast into place for all three members of the Squad.

Gus moved first. Striding into the casket room, he dived for the mummified cat and lifted it more roughly than you probably should lift a priceless ancient Egyptian moggy. As he turned it round, they could all see a shocking sight: a neat hole had been cut out of the back of the little mummy. Inside was just empty space, about the right size to hold a piece of chunky jewellery. Dust and threads spilled onto the floor from the hole.

This cat had been burgled!

"Vera Damclot did that! She's the thief!"

"But she's got away!"

"With the bracelet!"

"Is there still time to catch her?"

Before they could hatch a plan the toilet door in the

corridor banged, and the team spotted a familiar figure

walking past the entrance to the Egyptian Zone. It was

(so-called) Professor Peter Gyptex, and it looked like he was heading towards the museum exit. Quickly.

Gus whispered urgently, "Don't let him suspect we know what's going on. We need him, but we need to get Vera as well. He's bound to know where she is. They're in this together." Then in a much louder voice he called out, "Professor! Hallo, Professor Gyptex!"

The man froze, unsure at first who was calling to him. Then he turned and smiled, but the smile seemed forced, as though he was nervous and trying to hide it. "Hallo again! Er... good to see you. I've er... just been back to finish off a few things."

Gyptex looked particularly rosy-cheeked, as though he had just scrubbed his face. He held a bag that appeared to be full of clothes.

"We've had your friend in visiting the Egyptian Zone to look at the cat mummy," said Gus casually. "You've just missed her."

"Ah yes, Vera," said the so-called professor, managing to hold his grin. "She is quite a character." He moved the bag from one hand to the other.

"Have you seen her recently?" asked Laurie innocently.

"Er... no. I'm... um... sorry I missed her," said Gyptex rather vaguely. "Look, I'd love to talk further but I simply must head off. Plane to catch, you know?" The professor was about to check his watch, the big timepiece looking bumpy and bulky under his jacket sleeve, but then he seemed to think better of it.

"The casket has been a most interesting project,"

he continued. "I'll write up the information I've gathered and send a copy to the museum." He started walking briskly away. Without turning around he gave a backwards wave as he went, in an effort to finish the conversation cheerfully.

That gesture seems very familiar, thought Kennedy.

"Wait right here," said Gus to the Squad. "I just want to check the toilets." He strode through the door in the corridor just outside the Egyptian Zone, and was back out again in a matter of seconds clutching something. "Nothing suspicious, but he left this by mistake."

It was Peter Gyptex's huge watch.

"Hang on a minute," said Laurie. "If he's not wearing that, then why did he have such a big bumpy lump around his wrist?"

Two things happened at the same time.

Gus broke into a run. And Kennedy shouted:

"The bracelet!"

"After him!" roared Nabster.

"They must have switched it. Vera Damclot stole it from the cat; Peter Gyptex is going to get it out of the building!"

Chapter 10
In which there is a
chase for a bracelet

The team tore through the corridors once more. They had to stop Gyptex leaving the museum with the stolen bracelet.

What they needed was a shortcut and it was Kennedy who thought of it. "This way!" She took a sudden left turn through a door marked

STAFF ONLY

They were immediately in an empty echoing stairway.

There were no museum displays or visitors in their way. They had a direct route down to the main doors and a chance to get there before the thief.

"Hopefully he'll not be moving too quickly," said Laurie, "cause he won't want anyone to get suspicious."

They raced down the stairs, feet pattering like drumbeats. Kennedy's hair was flying as she went. Laurie's Indiana Jones hat fell off in the rush and was caught by Nabster. Gus strode down three steps at a time behind them all.

At the bottom, the Squad burst into the main foyer, right beside the museum's doors, but Gus paused in the stairwell to call the police and Museum Director Magda Gaskar. "I'll be right with you," he said.

Laurie, Nabster and Kennedy craned their necks to

see if their target was in view. Just as they had hoped, a tall figure in the distance was heading their way. Gyptex was approaching the exit, but they had got there first. He was doing his best to look like a normal visitor, pausing every now and then to glance at a display.

"How do we get him to stop?" asked Laurie.

"Where's Gus when you need him?" groaned Kennedy. "What do we do?"

It was Nabster who had the answer. He grabbed his bag and began pulling things out, though Kennedy found it hard to imagine how they could stop a thief with a pen and notebook or a measuring tape.

But as the fake professor got close to them, Nabster moved swiftly. He swung round and pointed the ScanRay at Gyptex like a gun, shouting, "HANDS UP!"

The man was so surprised by the command that he didn't even have time to think. His hands automatically shot into the air.

As his arms reached up, his sleeves stretched down– and on one of his wrists shone a beautiful, thick, gem-studded golden band.

"Pharaoh Shaneb's bracelet!"

"There it is!"

"We knew it!"

Gyptex dropped the bag he'd been carrying. A red wig spilled out, alongside a large cardigan with a cat picture on the back. Realising that he had stuck his hands in the air for little more than a supermarket scanner, the tall man quickly tried to pull back his sleeve. He made a desperate dive to refill the bag.

But it was too late.

Gus skidded to a stop beside them. He had arrived in time to spot the bracelet, and put a firm hand on the thief's shoulder. "Why's he got Vera Damclot's clothes?" He gave the Squad a confused look.

"For the same reason he waves like Vera Damclot and is the same height as her. For the same reason that they are both a little bit too interested in the casket and the cat," said Kennedy.

"Oh you think you'r-r-r-r-re so clever-r-r-r, don't yo-o-o-o-u." The voice was Vera Damclot's but it came from Peter Gyptex.

The cat lady and the professor were the same person.

"You mean Peter Gyptex *is* Vera Damclot?" asked Gus, bewildered.

"Yes. Two disguises, one thief, lots of confusion," said Kennedy.

"Or to put it in ancient Egyptian..." Nabster scribbled in his notebook:

"I think we have successfully solved the mystery of the hidden hieroglyphics," said Laurie.

"I think you have." It was Magda. She had arrived in time to see the jewellery thief's capture. "And I think that the Paris museum might want a little chat with whoever Peter-Vera really is. I have a funny feeling it wasn't a brother and sister who stole the other bracelet. There was another reason why the CCTV images looked alike." Magda was closely followed by the police. They had brought some different bracelets for the fake professor to wear: a nice set of handcuffs.

Last Chapter
In Which the Case is Closed

Kennedy's Diary

Wednesday, 4:00 p.m.

We've closed the file on the Case of the Hidden Hieroglyphics, so today we can have a rest. It's back to normal in here — but things are just a little bit different upstairs.

Pharaoh Shaneb's bracelet is in its very own display case. After thousands of years being bandaged up with a dead cat, everyone will have a chance to see it. I think Laurie is disappointed — he was hoping to wear it for a bit.

The Paris museum will be getting their bracelet back too, now that the crime has been solved.

A photo of the gleaming bracelet was on the smartboard at the HQ until Nabster put up a report from the local paper for them all to read. Kennedy looked up from her diary.

"The Pharaoh must have liked his cat an amazing amount to wrap it up with one of his most prized possessions," she said.

"Keep your voice down," warned Nabster. "If Colin hears you, he might expect to get his tiny paws on all of our most precious things!"

"In that case he'll be claiming your ScanRay," said Laurie.

"And Kennedy's diary," said Nabster.

"And Laurie's sleeping bag!" said Kennedy.

"Too late. Laurie's already wrapped inside that like some kind of mummy," said Nabster.

"Very funny," came Laurie's muffled voice.

"It says here that 'Professor Gyptex-Vera' has been locked away," said Nabster. "His real name is Paul Pitt."

The report showed a set of four pictures – the man and the woman who were the suspected thieves of the Paris bracelet robbery, and below them Peter Gyptex and Vera Damclot. All four were really the jewellery thief Paul Pitt. A final fifth picture showed him without any disguise on.

FOUR THIEVES REVEALED TO BE THE SAME PERSON!

JEWELLERY THIEF PAUL PITT IS BEHIND BARS AFTER A FOILED ATTEMPT TO RECREATE HIS PARIS MUSEUM THEFT IN EDINBURGH

Pitt had pretended to be two people in his successful theft in France and tried a similar crime yesterday at the capital's museum using two different disguises.

Dressed as cat-loving Vera Damclot he stole a priceless Egyptian bracelet from a mummified cat before hiding in the toilets and changing outfit. "His plan was that Vera would never be seen leaving the building," explained Museum Director Magda Gaskar. "Instead, dressed as Professor Peter Gyptex he would have walked out of the museum, seemingly a respected professor, but secretly wearing a valuable bracelet – a perfect plan, if the Museum Mystery Squad hadn't foiled it."

"I wonder if he cried for his mummy when he was told he was going to prison?" said Nabster with a smile. "Am I starting to sound like Gus?"

"Well, he can count the hours until he's free again with that nice big watch!" said Kennedy.

The team discussed the case a little more but soon turned to their own activities: sleeping, diary writing and puzzles.

"I'm think I'm getting better at these now," said Nabster. "Stone structure built in ancient Egypt. Seven letters, beginning with 'p'.

Pyramid. Easy. What's this one, though...? Two words, eight letters and three letters. A warm, padded, human-sized sack used as bedding."

There was a sigh and then a muffled voice from the sofa. "It's *sleeping bag*."

"Ohhhh yeaaaaah..." said Nabster happily.

NABSTER'S WORDSEARCH

Nabster is having some trouble with his wordsearch. Can you help him find all the hidden words? Answers at the back.

MUSEUM	SPHINX	BRACELET
MUMMY	CAT	SYMBOL
PYRAMID	TREASURE	PAPYRUS
PHARAOH	NILE	HEADDRESS

I	T	E	O	H	S	B	P	A	T
M	S	M	P	H	A	R	A	O	H
A	U	M	E	U	H	A	P	S	E
P	A	S	N	G	A	C	A	M	A
H	U	P	E	A	G	E	Y	F	D
A	X	H	S	U	I	L	T	A	D
E	N	I	L	E	M	E	R	U	R
S	L	N	A	I	N	T	E	L	E
M	S	X	R	A	D	R	A	S	S
P	Y	R	A	M	I	D	S	B	S
E	M	D	N	C	S	A	U	A	E
V	B	U	P	A	P	Y	R	U	S
G	O	E	M	T	E	S	E	B	E
A	L	O	S	M	O	R	A	H	P
T	R	E	A	S	Y	M	L	E	T

Mike Nicholson

Mike Phillips

Mike Nicholson is a bike rider, shortbread baker, bad juggler and ear wiggler, and author of the *Museum Mystery Squad* series among other books for children.

Mike Phillips learnt to draw by copying characters from his favourite comics. Now he spends his days drawing astronauts, pirates, crocodiles and other cool things.

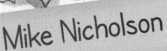

THE NEXT CASE...

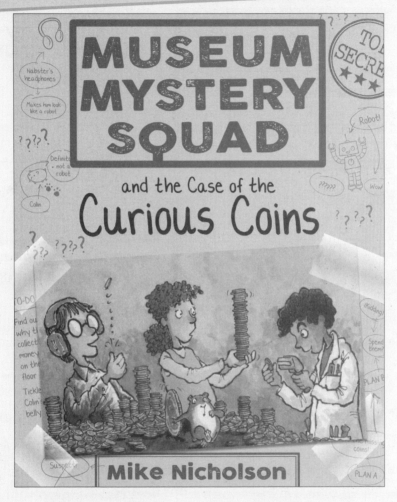

Missing money means trouble for the Squad. Will the penny drop before any more disappears?

ANSWERS

NABSTER'S WORDSEARCH
(Page 116)

I	T	E	O	H	S	B	P	A	T
M	S	M	P	H	A	R	A	O	H
A	U	M	E	U	H	A	P	S	E
P	A	S	N	G	A	C	A	M	A
H	U	P	E	A	G	E	Y	F	D
A	X	H	S	U	I	L	T	A	D
E	N	I	L	E	M	E	R	U	R
S	L	N	A	I	N	T	E	L	E
M	S	X	R	A	D	R	A	S	S
P	Y	R	A	M	I	D	S	B	S
E	M	D	N	C	S	A	U	A	E
V	B	U	P	A	P	Y	R	U	S
G	O	E	M	T	E	S	E	B	E
A	L	O	S	M	O	R	A	H	P
T	R	E	A	S	Y	M	L	E	T

DECODE HIEROGLYPHICS
(Page 58)

1. I love cats
2. Hamsters eat carrots
3. Laurie sleeps all the time
4. Kennedy writes a diary
5. Nabster thinks gadgets are cool
6. Dead pharaohs are found in pyramids

FACT OR FICTION?
(Page 86)

1. **TRUE**
2. **FALSE**, a sphinx has the head of a human and the body of a lion
3. **FALSE**, ordinary pyramids took approximately 10 years to build; the Great Pyramid at Giza took 20–30 years
4. **TRUE**
5. **TRUE**
6. **FALSE**, it's the symbol for water